Seekers of the Aweto

As this story unfolds, I feel like I'm sharing a big secret with you. The feeling surprises me and moves me. None of this would have been possible without the support of the Gallimard team, Wang Ning, Nicolas Grivel, and those close to me. I hope this new chapter will give you an incredible experience.

—Nie Jun

Story and art by Nie Jun

English-language translation by Edward Gauvin, with reference to the French translation and the original Chinese text
Additional translation assistance courtesy of Helen Chao

First American edition published in 2023 by Graphic Universe™
Published in arrangement with Gallimard Jeunesse and Sylvain Coissard Agency
Gallimard Jeunesse edition, *Aweto #2, La Traversée des steppes*, published in arrangement with Beijing Total Vision and Nicolas Grivel Agency. *Aweto #2, La Traversée des steppes* translated from the Chinese text by Soline Le Saux.

Graphic Universe™
An imprint of Lerner Publishing Group, Inc.
241 First Avenue North
Minneapolis, MN 55401 USA

For reading levels and more information, look up this title at www.lernerbooks.com.

Main body text set in Andy Std. Typeface provided by Monotype Typography.

Library of Congress Cataloging-in-Publication Data

Names: Jun, Nie, 1975– author, artist.
Title: Strange alliances / Nie Jun ; translated by Edward Gauvin.
Other titles: La Traversée des steppes. English
Description: First American edition. | Minneapolis : Graphic Universe, 2023. | Series: Seekers of the Aweto ; book 2 | Audience: Ages 12–18 | Audience: Grades 10–12 | Translated from the French. | Summary: "Xinyue, a hunter of rare treasures turned guardian of an infant deity, has escaped death. As the creature in his care grows in power, they begin a journey toward Xinyue's homeland"— Provided by publisher.
Identifiers: LCCN 2022033746 (print) | LCCN 2022033747 (ebook) | ISBN 9781541597853 (library binding) | ISBN 9781728478296 (paperback) | ISBN 9781728480800 (ebook)
Subjects: CYAC: Graphic novels. | Fantasy. | BISAC: YOUNG ADULT FICTION / Comics & Graphic Novels / Fantasy | YOUNG ADULT FICTION / Social Themes / Self-Esteem & Self-Reliance | LCGFT: Fantasy comics. | Graphic novels.
Classification: LCC PZ7.7.J83 St 2023 (print) | LCC PZ7.7.J83 (ebook) | DDC 741.5/973—dc23/eng/20220719

LC record available at https://lccn.loc.gov/2022033746
LC ebook record available at https://lccn.loc.gov/2022033747

Manufactured in the United States of America
1-47925-48370-9/16/2022

Seekers of the AWETO

2. Strange Alliances

NIE JUN

Translated by Edward Gauvin

with assistance from Helen Chao

Graphic Universe™ • Minneapolis

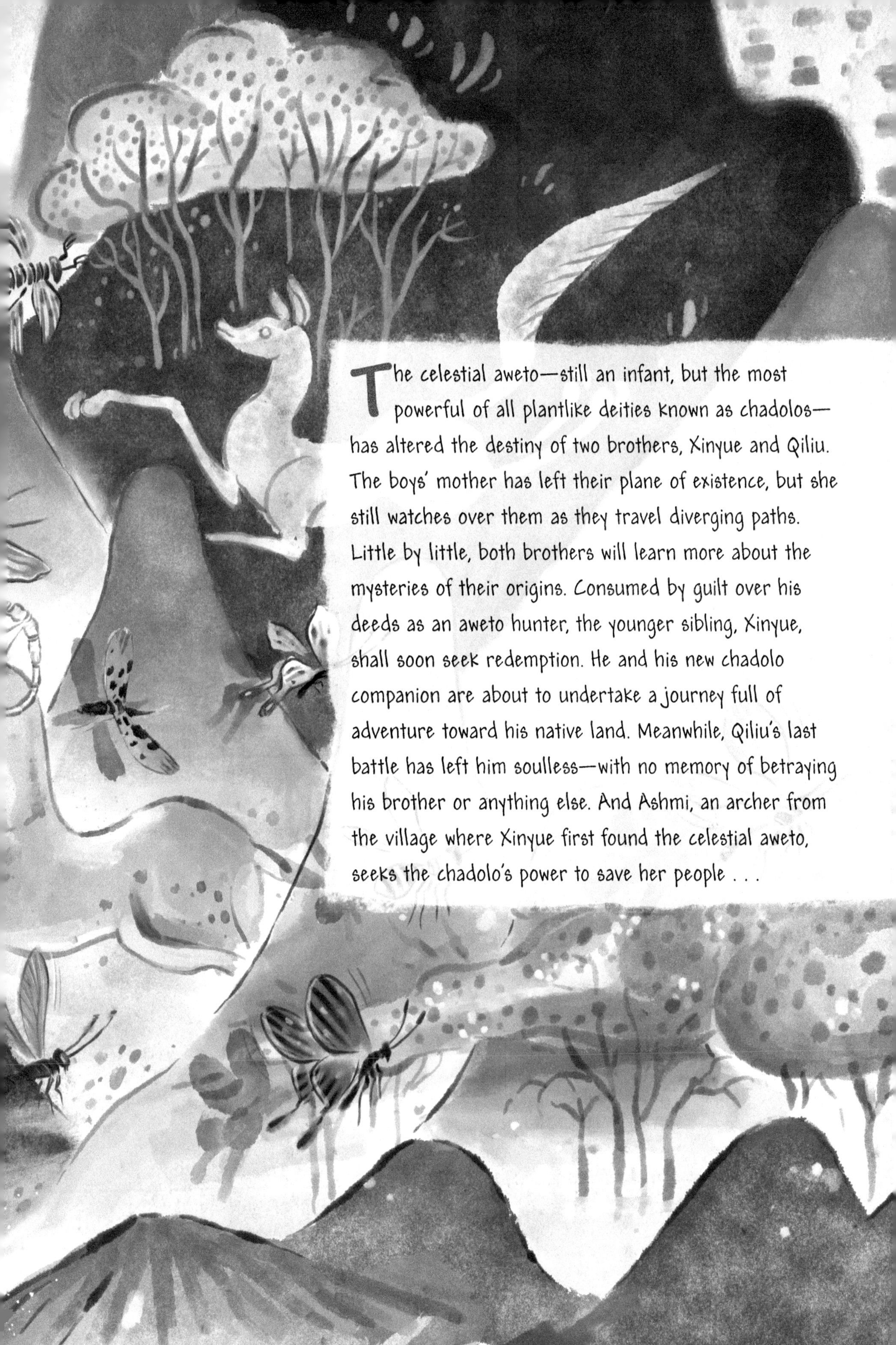

The celestial aweto—still an infant, but the most powerful of all plantlike deities known as chadolos—has altered the destiny of two brothers, Xinyue and Qiliu. The boys' mother has left their plane of existence, but she still watches over them as they travel diverging paths. Little by little, both brothers will learn more about the mysteries of their origins. Consumed by guilt over his deeds as an aweto hunter, the younger sibling, Xinyue, shall soon seek redemption. He and his new chadolo companion are about to undertake a journey full of adventure toward his native land. Meanwhile, Qiliu's last battle has left him soulless—with no memory of betraying his brother or anything else. And Ashmi, an archer from the village where Xinyue first found the celestial aweto, seeks the chadolo's power to save her people . . .

And their mama, Bu Ren Niang, was a revenant, huh? She'd stayed on this earth to look after her children instead of fading away . . .

Still waiting for you to mix those colors!

Had I known it would prove so distracting, I'd never have told you that tale!

Master, you said once that losing your soul means losing your memory too. What happened to the older brother, then?

Will he ever get them back?

In the Western Steppes, lost souls drift toward the Warm Sea. The only way to recover a soul is to strike a deal with the Soul Merchant.

What about Xinyue? Is he still alive? Will he ever find his way home?

Heaven and Earth are home to ten thousand things. We make companions of both light and shadow . . .

A drifter's life is like a dream. What joy to roam to and fro! But time passes for travelers too. Powerless, we see it go . . .

A drifter's life is like a dream. What joy . . .

Oh! Sigh.

Where'd you come from?
Awake at last, are we?

Who are you?
Answer me!
D-don't hurt me!
I can explain!
Start talking!
Where am I?
You're rash.
Far too rash!

Your voice . . . are you from Can Tianjin?

Yes! I am Miaodeng, from the capital's high religious court. I followed Master Yiting to the Southern Celestial Kingdom on a pilgrimage of knowledge. Our path led us here . . . I'll explain.

Miaodeng: lamp of wonders;
Yiting: one who listens

Quick, Miaodeng, sketch his likeness! They're a rare sight indeed!

Hah!
Heh heh!

You're mine now! Croak!

I'll bring you to my king. He'll pardon me and let me come home!

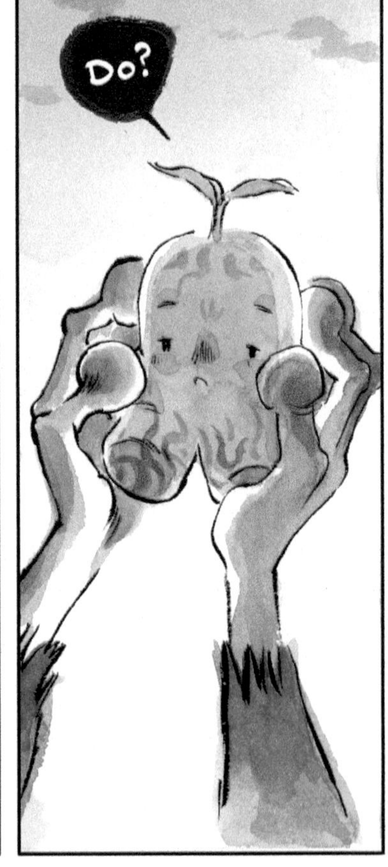
Do?

The kid I'll sell to a wolf ravager. That'll keep me in coin for the road! Croak!

Huh!?

Aaa!

Quit your crying!

Come back here!

A sandstorm! Master, listen . . . someone's in distress!
Those cries! That's the fabled earthen tongue!
Pant! Master Yiting . . . help!
Miaodeng, fear not! If you can't find me after the storm . . .
Look to your heartlight. Understand?
Yes . . . Master!

Aaaah!

What are you saying?

Hnnngh!
Heavy!

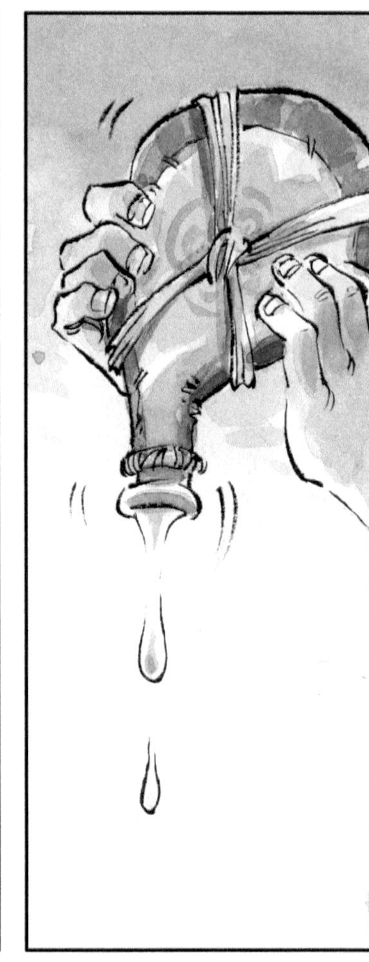

He's bleeding . . .

You just . . .
he's . . .

Huh?

. . . And now **I'm** here. But my brother, my mother . . .
Where is the chadolo?

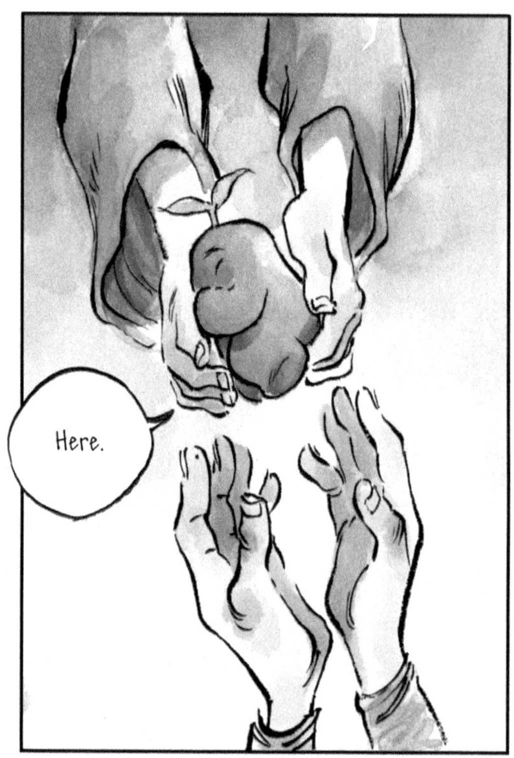
Here.

He healed your wound, then fell asleep.
The wound . . . my brother gave me.
I have to go!

Take me with you! Please don't leave me alone.

I'm an aweto seeker, and a cursed one at that. It'd be too dangerous!

Fine, I'll level with you. We absconded with the heartlight from Can Tianjin, and there's no going back!

The clouds . . . Mother? Is that a sign?

Oh, this is all my fault! I have sinned!

Don't like hyena, eh? Great, I'll make jerky with the leftovers.

So **this** is a heartlight?

It is linked to the lights in the hearts of all others who believe.
All others?

It never goes out?

Gaze inside. Anyone with a heartlight can hear you, no matter where they are or what language they speak.
Want to try? Tell Master Yiting your name.
Oh! I'm . . . Xinyue.

Xinyue, please watch over Miaodeng for me . . .
Huh!?

Your heart will show you the way. Head for the most beautiful land of all: your own.

Will I ever find it?

Deep in the woods where flowers blossom by the thousand . . .

. . . lies the peaceful and beautiful land of Qiemi.

A Qiemi marauder! At death's door, they play the flute of tears.

Travelers! Do you seek the celestial aweto?

What did you say?
I had the honor of seeing it!

Where!?
The baby chadolo is headed to Qiemi land.
Take this, my flute of tears. All my secrets are contained in its melody.
Only **it** can guide you to the celestial aweto . . .

Haha! Remember, Qiliu . . .

Ggkkh!
Your soul is headed for the Soul Merchant of the Warm Sea!
I'll barter to get it back—but only if you get me that celestial aweto!
Cough! Gkh!
Hey! What's the meaning of this?
FIUU!

Don’t let him get away!

Tianzhao: red-maned beings believed to be half human and half animal

I'll gut this crooked merchant!
Hah! Take this!
Ow! It burns!
So itchy!

Hemlock powder from the Western Sea. Expensive stuff.
Without an antidote, you'll rot down to your marrow.

You . . . poisoned us!?
Why were you shouting about the celestial aweto?

You've got sharp ears. A Qiemi marauder stole the young chadolo. We're going after it.
A Qiemi . . . ? The flute player! He was telling the truth!

You lot look clever. And I could use some guides. In exchange, I'll give you the antidote.

Looks like we're hostages . . .
We accept!
Then it's a deal! I'm a man of my word. Here's a first dose.
Now let's make camp for the night.
If these fools have transit papers, we can move more quickly in their company . . . till we get what we need.
Good plan.

The land of the Qiemi is in the Forest of Poison Mists.

Once we reach it, we can go our separate ways.

SLOP!

Eat up, brute!

Who knows what's become of our tribe? We must stay strong for their sake.
Look at that aweto seeker. He's lost his wits!

Cough! Blegh!

PLOP!

Guh?

Suffering makes you look almost human. You truly can't remember a thing?

You're better off not trying to retrieve it.

Qiliu!
It's me, Houlmet!
Young man, I think we're positioned to make a deal.
Huh . . . ?
Get up, wastrel! Don't just lay about!
Who . . . am . . .
PA
Aggh!
PA!

Stop.
And I thought you needed him to find the chadolo. Now let's get moving!
What an upstart! Remember, I give the orders around here!
You've struck him enough already.
I've got transit papers for the fastest routes. In a week, we'll be in Qiemi land.

MMM!
KSHANA 刹那

What do you think? Can I call you Kshana?
ksha ne!

Whaa . . .?

This wasn't here before my nap. Did you make the tree bear fruit?

What are you writing?
Just now, through the heartlight, my master gave our little friend a name!
Kshana, is it?
And what's that?
Oh, I buried the hyena so its soul could rest in peace.
If not for my sins, I'd be starving! And now there's nothing left for jerky!
Hey, hold on! I did it to help cleanse you of your sins!!

Who's starving? We've got plenty of delicious pomegranates! See? When we do good deeds, we're rewarded.

Keep 'em. I'm a carnivore!

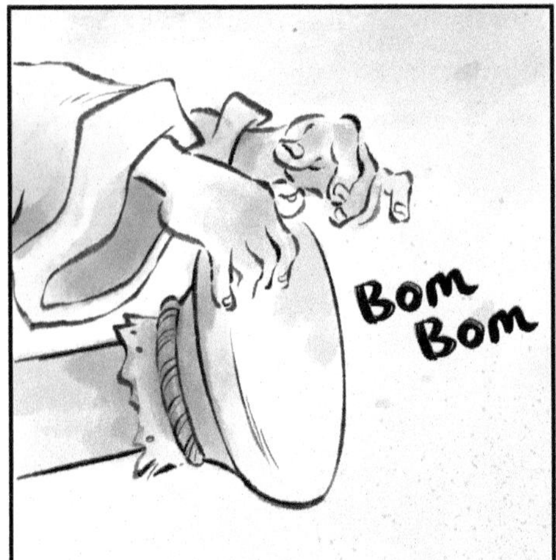

trundle
trundle

Look!
The drum's making
the butterflies
come to me!
Bom
Bom

I know her! That's Princess Anxi of Can Tianjin. She's off to be wed to a foreigner.
I've seen her before. But how'd she get **my** drum?
trundle
trundle

Stop bashing it like that! You'll rile up the insects!
Huh?

As I said—far too rash!

Oof!

Get back, you little ruffian!
Swipe

Now, now, Koulun. Manners! That drum must belong to the boy.
It's mine now. Finders keepers!
You're being very haughty, princess!
I said, **finders keepers!**
Heh!
Princess Anxi is famously willful.
I'll show her! She's not in her palace anymore . . .

Look! What's that? Another new toy?
Where?

Fsshh

Something's moving under the sand!
Sit back and enjoy the show. Dilongs are coming.

Grrr . . .

Looks like trouble. Get the princess to safety!
I'm perfectly safe here with Koulun. I'm staying!
Fsshhh
Nyaaak!
Fwoosh
Everybody run!

You're up,
Koulun!

Yeah!
Get 'em!
Back, earth
dragons!
POW
Ny-
oww!

My drum!

What's our plan?
Stay put!
. . . And watch the princess get to know the dilongs.
Huh?? We have to help!
Arrgh!
Nyaaak!
They just keep coming!
Princess, I—
Nyaaak!

Bzzzz
Wraak!
This is no time to play your drum!
You want to save them, right?
So let's have some fun.
Fun? **Now?**

See? Lots of fun.

Bom Bom Boom Boom

They'll leave once they've had enough.

What wizardry!
FFssh

Huh.
Don't fret, Auntie Hu.
Oh, thank goodness you're all right, Princess!

Hey, which way are you going? Wanna come with us?

Pssh.
Taking in strays now that you lost your toy?
I won't say no!

Little barbarian! Don't think just 'cause you know magic you get to be rude!
Hands off, you lunkhead!

Hmph!

Would fruit tarts help?

Say . . .
. . . what?

Ooo . . .

Hands off!
For guests, not
castoffs from
the One-Eyed.

The young princess
picked them out
especially for you.
Enjoy!

What'd I tell you? Good deeds get rewarded!

Hrrmph!

Hear that? The guard's from the One-Eyed People—but born with two eyes! Quite rare.

So he can't eat these? Snobs.

Here. I'm Xinyue.

For me? Koulun?

Yumm!!

They can't be **that** good.
Mmmm . . .

I've always had to steal to eat.

Does it taste sweeter stolen?
What?

This is the first time anyone's **gifted** me food.
MMM

Hey! You already had a taste, glutton!
Yummy yum yum!

Spit it out!

Excuse me?

This is the princess's private bath tent!
Rogues! I should have you imprisoned.

We'll be crossing Youzhi land to get to Suye and my betrothed.
Take that, rogue!
Suye? My master has spoken of it.
Oh? Come with us and I'll pardon you for barging into the bath tent.
Is that a threat?
go go

So it was that Xinyue, Kshana, and Miaodeng joined the caravan of Princess Anxi on the road to Youzhi . . .

Three days later, southeast of the Western Steppes

Forest of Poison Mists, here we come!
The flute of tears is vibrating. It can tell we're close to its home.
hummm
The Qiemi, and the chadolo, must be hidden within.

Ashmi! Qiliu! You go in and scout.

What? We should stick together!

Fine.

Remember!
Find me that aweto, and I'll fulfill your heart's desire, be it for more antidote or your soul.

If I don't make it back, you two keep searching for the chadolo.

We'll give you till sundown. Then we're going in!

Don't come back without that aweto!

Listen! Hear the flute of tears? It's giving us the way.
Toooroooo
Find it . . . or else!

Ashmi, do you think the flute holds secrets about me?
We'll know once we've found the Messenger. For now, hush!

What's wrong?
Shh!

It's too quiet.

Ash . . . mi . . .
What the—!?

Slash
You fool!
Why didn't you yell for help?
You told me to be quiet.

HUU~

Up ahead! No choice . . .

Jump!

Ashmi!

Oh, no! The flute!

Wait—I can hear it!

It must be leading us to the Messenger . . .

We'll unlock that song's secrets yet!

All these years, I have beheld thee.

I've aged, but you remain as beautiful as ever!

Hmm?

Whose flute of tears is that, ruining my wistful mood?

Sh-thok!
Croak!

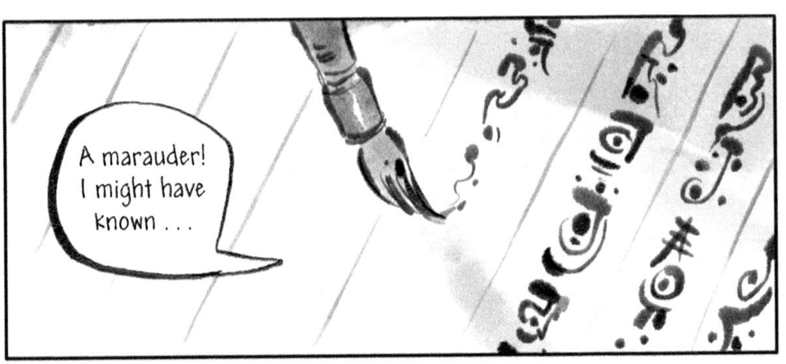
A marauder! I might have known . . .

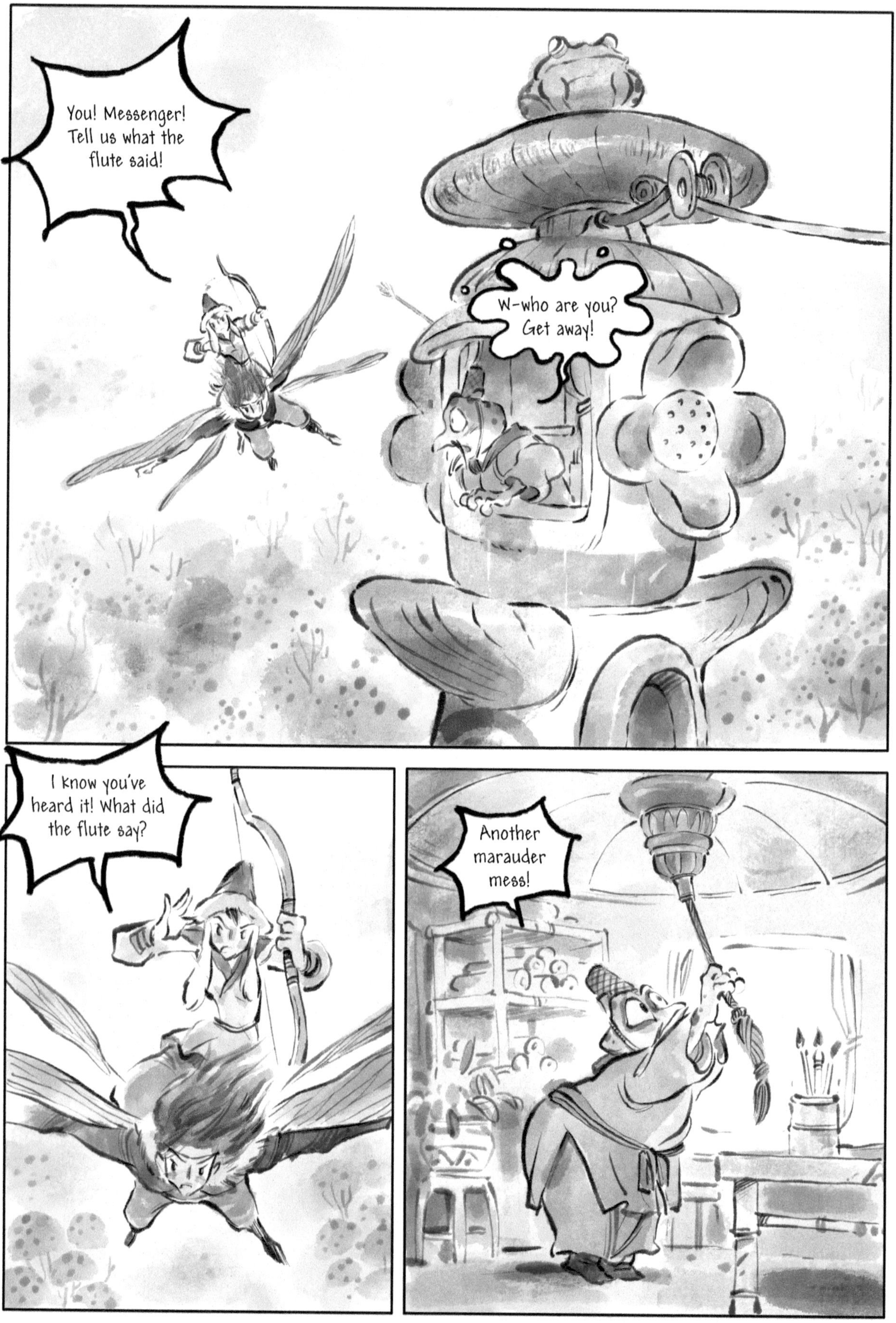

You! Messenger! Tell us what the flute said!

W-who are you? Get away!

Gasp! Pant! Oh, I'm too old for this!

Huh?

Hello there!
Looks like newlyweds!
Come try my tea!

That's a rare sight!
We haven't had visitors in ages.
This deserves a song, for our friends from afar!

Deep in the wood where ten thousand flowers bloom, Qiemi land welcomes you . . .
As we sing and dance, let this land of ours enchant you . . .
Fancy a drink, Messenger?
Can't you see I'm busy!?

Long time, no see, Messenger! What's your hurry?

Soused on the job, huh? Is His Majesty around?

For too long, we have endured the poor reputation our marauders have brought upon us!
But why must we be cut off from the world?
I feel a duty to leave—to be an ambassador to other lands! Let them learn to love and accept us!
Croak?
Forgive me. I didn't mean to interrupt the prince's brilliant speech.
BLAM

Huh!?
These ruffians just forced their way in!
Oh?
A chadolo! Where is it? The marauder knew of its path . . .
What is it you want?
A marauder's flute of tears led them here.
Those sly marauders!

I'd **never** let a marauder return here. So before dying, they hide **their souls** in their flutes and **trick people** into bringing them back to us.
There **is no** chadolo in my kingdom. You've been **deceived!**
What? How can it be?
Begone, fools!

You won't get rid of us that easily!
Argh . . . Papa! Croak!

Psst! I'm happy to be a hostage—just swear you'll take me with you!

My child!
Command your Messenger—tell us what the flute said!

My tribe is almost dead. I beg of you. I just want him to tell me where the chadolo is!
Easy now!

Messenger! What are you **waiting** for?

Ahem. I, Messenger, swear to the gods to faithfully interpret the flute's tune.

"In the Yumen market . . ."

"I saw a pair of brothers with a chadolo. Its leaves gave off a golden light. It could only have been . . ."
". . . the celestial aweto!"

"The elder brother, Qiliu, seized upon the aweto and took his sword to the younger brother, Xinyue."
"I spat out a deadly gas, enough to make the elder brother's soul leave his body, then stole away with the aweto and Xinyue."
The boys' mother told him he belongs there.
"If Xinyue still breathes, he will surely head for the lands of Youzhi."
"As I hurried back to Qiemi, I upset the chadolo. He summoned a sandstorm, burying me."
Brother . . . did I kill him over . . . an aweto?

Nonsense! It can't be!
The messenger can't lie!
He swore before the gods.
Grr . . . **Scoundrels!** Do you take us for **marauders?**
Aaaah...
Croak! Papa can't stand marauders! He's about to blow!

This way! Jump!

Crr... Oaakk!!!

Baokeli, **my son!** Where are you **going!?**

The brave little prince begins a mysterious adventure . . .
Packing hope and courage inside his bags . . .
Boom!
Foolish boy! When you learn what the outside world is like, **you'll regret this!**
Farewell, father! Await my return!
And I will prove the justness of my cause!

Sigh. By now those two wastrels **must** be dead.
No sign of Ashmi.
Have faith.

Hey! It's her!
Yoo-hoo! Ashmi!

Greetings!
Well? What treasures have you brought me?

What have you found, Ashmi?

The marauder tricked us into bringing his soul back to his homeland.

What? He duped us?

Another seeker may have the chadolo. We must go to Youzhi at once!

Youzhi!?

Did you think this **thing** would appease me? Hmpf!
Croak!
Punt
Aaaa . . .
Hm? Qiliu?
You knew I'd lost my memory! Why didn't you tell me about my brother!?
Ingrate! Have you gone mad?
Ack! Remember! I'll barter . . . for your soul!
I'm sick of your promises!

Enough. If your brother's alive, he's headed for Youzhi.

With . . . the celestial aweto?
Xinyue . . .

I really **was** a villain . . .

I don't think you're a villain!

What the . . .

On to Youzhi. In case that little aweto seeker still lives.

The White Colt Border Post is only the way through. But I've got safe passage!

The lands of Youzhi are our only hope now.
Look out, world, here I come!
Croak! Away we go!
Stay alive, little chadolo!
Don't even think of trying to ditch me! I've got more antidote— **and** the transit papers!

Let's stop for a break!
I need to stretch my legs!
Princess Anxi!

Careful, young princess . . .
Whee, these flowers are so beautiful!

A tiaosen!

A what?
An insect. It can sense danger.

See? Over there! A battle of some sort.

Diana, milady . . .

I'm coming!

I need a new goblet . . .

Ooof!
Bam

Urk!
Huh?

Heh.

Yay, Koulun!
Wow.

Don't be scared. I'm Koulun.
Qiu Wanjin. And I'm not.

Hey! Are you . . . like me?
From the One-Eyed People?

Why . . . yes.

Huh?
Your love life can wait!

AWoo AWoo
Kill them all! No one escapes!
Groaar!

We've got wolf ravagers incoming!

Groar!

Watch out!

Whoa, what's going on!?

FWOosh

Oof! Qiushe land! You?

Where do you call home now?

Can Tianjin.

Hm?

Huh?

The ground's . . . shaking?

Amazing!

It's like a giant rhinoceros beetle!

Kshana! Wait!

You're full of surprises!

They're circling back around!

Uh-oh!

A chadolo? I'll take it! Prepare to fall before wolf-ravager Jiao Mi!

Awoo!

All right—chaaarge!

Ngh!
Take that!
GAAA!!!

May the gods protect you!

What!? The leopard style of Youzhi?!
Raaargh!
None of your business, old wolf!
FWOOSH
Ungh!
THOKK

This way!

Urrkh . . .

Princess, where are you?
The ravagers are fleeing!

Cough!

The beetle got small!

Aw. Its front horn broke off.

Diana? Diana!! Milady!?

Weep not, Wanjin!
Huh?

I fell off the wolf's back, and this princess saved me.
People aren't lying when they say Qiushe women are the prettiest in all the world!
I'd like to extend hospitality to our rescuers.

The White Colt
Border Post
Can't we stop? I need a break!
Hold on, Houlmet. It'll be dark soon.
I see gates ahead! After White Colt, Youzhi's not far!

Look!
Over there!
Huh?

He's hurt!

Do . . .
I . . .
Badly wounded! **Help him!**

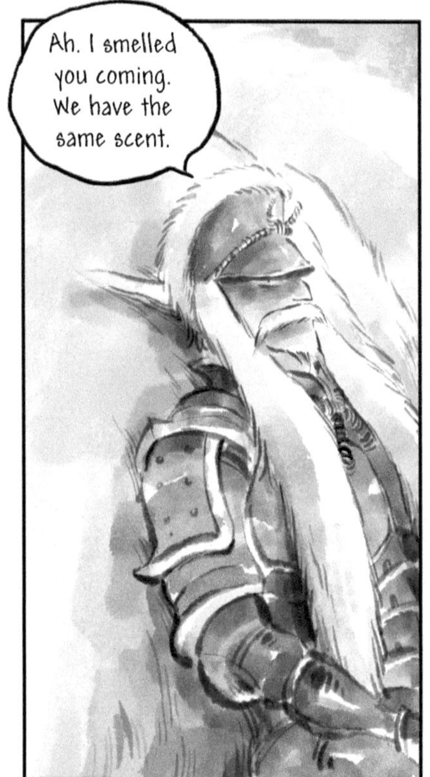
Ah. I smelled you coming. We have the same scent.

Do I know you?
Hm. I've lain with many women in the Western Steppes . . .

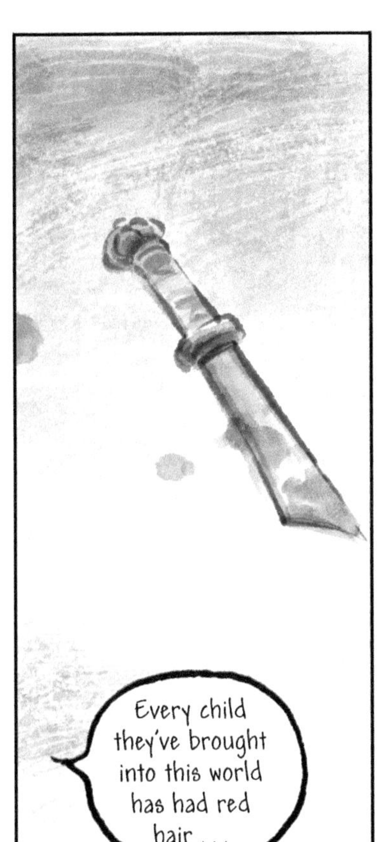
Every child they've brought into this world has had red hair . . .

Friend Qiliu, is this your kin?
I . . . can't remember.

Hmm! Now where can I find some . . .

A-ha! There!

If you are . . . I never stopped looking . . .
Cough! Your eyes . . . you've lost your soul, haven't you?

Chomp, chomp!

munch munch munch

Burp!

Here! A Qiemi remedy to stop your bleeding.
Cough . . .

YAAA

Oh, no!

Wolf ravagers!

Gallop

What's your name? Where are you going?
Qiliu. And Youzhi.
I am Jiao Mi, ravager of the wild Shou River. We shall meet again, Qiliu.
Wherever you go, your homeland watches over you. Your den is there.
Then I'll . . . see you someday?
Don't forget about me! I'm Baokeli!

Here, take this.
What is it?

The eye of home.

Watch out!
What?

FIUUU

Friend Qiliu!
My son!

Gallop

What have you done!?

I think that was Qiliu's father!
His father . . .? A wolf ravager?
My, what a pelt on that wolf! Worth its weight in gold!
Forgive me! Is there hope of saving him?
I've seen this knife before. It's . . . that kid's!
Cough! That means . . . Xinyue **is** alive!

Lost child, you have drifted far. Look north with your eye to the homeland!
Home . . . land . . .

You lost your way and lost your soul . . .

But someday you'll return to your own land . . .

Oh!
Is anyone there?
Where am I?

Can anyone hear me?
Father!
Is this . . .

. . . my home?

Oh, let me return!

WOO...

AWOO...

I want to be the boy I once was!

AWETO

To be continued . . .

The Art of Zhi
The people of Youzhi are the only to have mastered the secret art of zhi. Simply by beating a drum, they can summon and control insects of all sorts.

Mi Insects
These flying desert insects can pick up the trail of a chadolo thanks to their sharp hearing and keen vision.

Gu Insects
Also known as tiaosen, these insects can order their venomous larva to attack enemies.

Sheng Insects
Insects capable of healing wounds and finding food and water for their masters.

Luan Butterflies
Butterflies that can lead travelers astray and induce hallucinations.

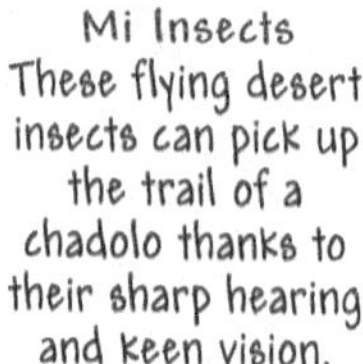

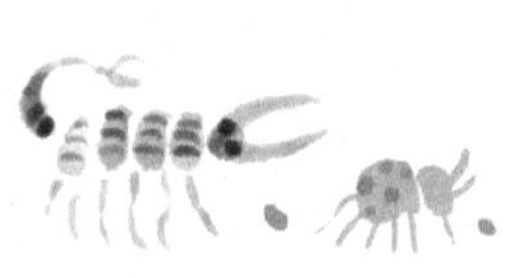

The People of Youzhi
In an ancient land in the middle of the Western Steppes, renowned for its beauty and lush flora, has lived this warm and welcoming people. They have mastered the art of zhi and can speak the earthen tongue.

The Sanamo People of Little Huoxun
A matriarchal tribe exiled from the ancient land of Huoxun. Sanamo women are valiant warriors. With the help of a chadolo, they had succeeded in leading a quiet life until recently.

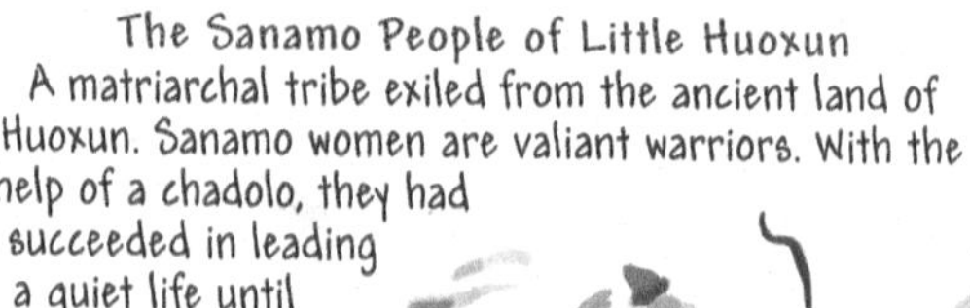

The Painters of Duhuang
These painters make frescoes using natural pigments in Duhuang Cave. They come from many countries and take inspiration from many cultures, employing artisanal techniques a thousand years old, passed down through generations. Some spend their whole lives painting in this cave.

Qiemi Marauders
Bandits guilty of cruel crimes, banished from the mysterious land of the Qiemi. They have mastered countless deadly techniques.

The Tianzhao
Children born of a wolf-ravager father and a human mother. Believed to live in the north of the Western Steppes.

The Yutian Art
A magical practice that allows one to fly with the help of giant insect wings.

Aweto Seekers
Aweto seekers sell herblike awetos to survive. And they employ all manner of schemes and devices to capture chadolos, the earth deities that produce awetos. Also known as aweto stealers, starpickers, and roam-crows.

Merchants of the Western Steppes
Striking deals from the Dashi land of the Western Sea to the capital of Can Tianjin, these merchants change their identities in the course of their journeys. Some purchase awetos at exorbitant prices, hoping one day to get their hands on the celestial aweto. Houlmet is one such merchant.

Qiemi Princeling, Sixteenth of His Name
Eighteen-year-old Baokeli is the sixteenth princeling of the Qiemi kingdom. Highly knowledgeable and cultured, he can bring out the healing properties of substances by chewing them.

The One-Eyed People
A mysterious, cycloptic tribe local to the Western Steppes. Members abandon all children born with two eyes.

The Messenger
The Messenger is an underpaid gatekeeper of the Qiemi kingdom. His main task is to interpret the words that Qiemi frogs who venture beyond their homeland confide to their flutes. The Messenger must extract information from these words.

Wolf Ravagers
These merciless warriors with snow-white coats dwell on the banks of the Shou River in the icy northern wastes of the Western Steppes. For years, they have been embroiled in constant conflicts while expanding their territory.

The Land of the Aweto Seekers

North
West
East
Land of the
Wolf Ravagers
South
Dingxi Checkpoint
Gechang
Great Wall
Open Market
of Yumen
Baiju
Checkpoint
Jiayu
Duhuang
Can Tianjin
Gobi Desert
Village of the
Sanamo Tribe
Place of the
Baby Chadolo's Discovery
Anning

About the Author

Nie Jun was born in 1975 in Xining, in the province of Qinghai, China. He began drawing at an early age by copying *lianhuanhua* (traditional Chinese palm-sized picture books of sequential art). He soon became a fan of Osamu Tezuka, Zhang Leping, and black-and-white pirated editions of *Tintin*. As a teenager, he won a contest sponsored by a comics magazine and had his drawings published for the first time. Later, he was deeply influenced by the range of works within the Chinese comics scene, as well as by Japanese artists Akira Toriyama and Katsuhiro Otomo, not to mention Moebius (the French cartoonist Jean Giraud). In 1995 he began to publish his art in magazines. He lives in Beijing and teaches drawing to university students. In 2018 the first English-language translation of his work, *My Beijing: Four Stories of Everyday Wonder*, arrived in the United States. It received a Mildred L. Batchelder Honor and a Will Eisner Comic Industry Awards nomination for Best US Edition of International Material—Asia.

About the Translator

Award-winning translator Edward Gauvin specializes in contemporary comics and fantastical fiction. As an advocate for translators and translated literature, he has written widely and spoken at universities and festivals. The translator of more than 425 graphic novels, he is a contributing editor for comics at *Words Without Borders*. His past collaborations with Lerner, ranging in setting from Lebanon to World War II France to modern-day Beijing, have been honored by the American Library Association and the Eisner Awards, and he is thrilled to be working with them again. Home is wherever his wife and daughter are.